Phonics Friends

Holly and Hank's Snow Holiday
The Sound of **H**

The Child's World

By Joanne Meier and Cecilia Minden

The Child's World

Published in the United States of America
by The Child's World®
PO Box 326
Chanhassen, MN 55317-0326
800-599-READ
www.childsworld.com

A special thank you to the Vargas and Clark families.
Gil and Grace, you made building a snowman fun!

The Child's World®: Mary Berendes, Publishing Director

Editorial Directions, Inc.: E. Russell Primm, Editorial
Director and Project Editor; Katie Marsico, Associate
Editor; Judith Shiffer, Associate Editor and School Media
Specialist; Linda S. Koutris, Photo Researcher and
Selector

The Design Lab: Kathleen Petelinsek, Design and Page
Production

Photographs ©: Photo setting and photography by Romie
and Alice Flanagan/Flanagan Publishing Services

Library of Congress Cataloging-in-Publication Data
Meier, Joanne D.
  Holly and Hank's snow holiday : the sound of H /
by Joanne Meier and Cecilia Minden.
    p. cm. — (Phonics friends)
  Holly helps Hank build a snowman, in simple text
featuring the "h" sound.
  ISBN 1-59296-296-3 (library bound : alk. paper)
[1. English language—Phonetics. 2. Reading.] I. Minden,
Cecilia. II. Title. III. Series.
PZ7.M5148Ho 2004
[E]—dc22   2004002195

Note to parents and educators:

The Child's World® has created Phonics Friends with the goal of exposing children to engaging stories and pictures that assist in phonics development. The books in the series will help children learn the relationships between the letters of written language and the individual sounds of spoken language. This contact helps children learn to use these relationships to read and write words.

The books in this series follow a similar format. An introductory page, to be read by an adult, introduces the child to the phonics feature, or sound, that will be highlighted in the book. Read this page to the child, stressing the phonic feature. Help the student learn how to form the sound with her mouth. The Phonics Friends story and engaging photographs follow the introduction. At the end of the story, word lists categorize the feature words into their phonic element. Additional information on using these lists is on The Child's World® Web site listed at the top of this page.

Each book in this series has been carefully written to meet specific readability requirements. Close attention has been paid to elements such as word count, sentence length, and vocabulary. Readability formulas measure the ease with which the text can be read and understood. Each Phonics Friends book has been analyzed using the Spache readability formula. For more information on this formula, as well as the levels for each of the books in this series please visit The Child's World® Web site.

Reading research suggests that systematic phonics instruction can greatly improve students' word recognition, spelling, and comprehension skills. The Phonics Friends series assists in the teaching of phonics by providing students with important opportunities to apply their knowledge of phonics as they read words, sentences, and text.

This is the letter *h*.

In this book, you will read words that have the *h* sound as in:

home, helping, hands, and *hat.*

Holly and Hank are home

from school.

They are making a snowman!

Holly is helping Hank.

"Here, use your hands like this," says Holly. "This is how you roll the snow."

Hank rolls three heavy snowballs.

He carries them to Holly.

"Now he needs a hat on his head," says Holly. Hank puts his hat on the snowman's head.

"Let's give him a happy face," says Holly.

"Here!" says Hank. "Here are some buttons."

Hank helps Holly make

a button face.

The snowman is done.

"Let's take him home!"

says Hank.

"The snowman has to stay here," says Holly. "He is too heavy to move. Bye-bye!"

Fun Facts

You wave your hand when you want to say hello or good-bye, and you might clap your hands when you applaud for a performer on stage. But some people use their hands to communicate all of the time. People who are deaf learn to spell with their hands or move their hands in a certain way to express themselves.

People have been wearing hats for a very long time! The remains of Egyptian mummies reveal that ancient people frequently wore hats and headdresses. People wear hats today to shade their eyes from the sun or to keep their heads warm. Thousands of years ago hats symbolized much more. At that time, the type of hat a person wore showed whether that individual was rich or poor, powerful or not important.

Activity

Learning How to Talk with Your Hands

Even if you don't know someone who is deaf, you still might enjoy learning sign language. Your local library should have several books with illustrations that show the different hand signs and what they mean. Ask a friend to learn the signs with you. That way, you can practice speaking with one another.

To Learn More

Books
About the Sound of H
Flanagan, Alice. *Hats Can Help: The Sound of H*. Chanhassen, Minn.: The
   Child's World, 2000.

About Hands
Penn, Audrey, Ruth E. Harper, and Nancy M. Leak. *The Kissing Hand*.
   Washington, D.C.: The Child Welfare League of America, 1993.
Ross, Tony. *Wash Your Hands*. Brooklyn: Kane/Miller, 2000.

About Hats
Brett, Jan. *The Hat*. New York: Putnam, 1997.
Brumbeau, Jeff, and Gail de Marcken. *Miss Hunnicutt's Hat*. New York:
   Orchard Books, 2003.

About Helping
Andreasen, Dan. *With a Little Help from Daddy*. New York: M. K. McElderry
   Books, 2003.
Spafford, Suzy. *Helping-Out Day?: Hooray!*. New York: Scholastic, 2003.

Web Sites
Visit our home page for lots of links about the Sound of H:

http://www.childsworld.com/links.html

Note to Parents, Teachers, and Librarians: We routinely check our Web links to make
sure they're safe, active sites—so encourage your readers to check them out!

H Feature Words

Proper Names
Hank

Holly

Feature Words in Initial Position
hand

happy

has

hat

he

head

heavy

help

helping

here

him

his

home

how

About the Authors

Joanne Meier, PhD, has worked as an elementary school teacher and university professor. She earned her BA in early childhood education from the University of South Carolina, and her MEd and PhD in education from the University of Virginia. She currently works as a literacy consultant for schools and private organizations. Joanne Meier lives with her husband Eric, and spends most of her time chasing her two daughters, Kella and Erin, and her two cats, Sam and Gilly, in Charlottesville, Virginia.

Cecilia Minden, PhD, directs the Language and Literacy Program at the Harvard Graduate School of Education. She is a reading specialist with classroom and administrative experience in grades K–12. She earned her PhD in reading education from the University of Virginia. Cecilia and her husband Dave Cupp enjoy sharing their love of reading with their granddaughter Chelsea.